A Place for Angels

CLYDE ROBERT BULLA

A Place
for Angels

Bu 1

pictures by JULIA NOONAN

BridgeWater Books

6791

Published by BridgeWater Books, an imprint of Troll Associates, Inc.

Printed in the United States of America.

10   9   8   7   6   5   4   3   2   1

Library of Congress Cataloging-in-Publication

Bulla, Clyde Robert.
A place for angels / by Clyde Robert Bulla;
illustrated by Julia Noonan.
p.   cm.
Summary: Claudine's father creates an angel that looks like her
dead mother and then a series of angel sculptures that take on a
special significance for her when she goes to live with her aunt
after her father's death.
ISBN 0-8167-3662-6
[1. Fathers and daughters—Fiction. 2. Artists—Fiction.
3. Aunts—Fiction. 4. Orphans—Fiction.]   I. Noonan, Julia, ill.
II. Title.
PZ7.B912Pl   1995   [Fic]—dc20   94-34219

For Barb,
no stranger to angels
C.B.

With love to Shelly and Marcia Sacks
J.N.

Contents

CHAPTER ONE

Where Is It Written?

It began on that rainy afternoon toward the end of winter. Claudine had walked home from school. Her hair was wet, and she was a little cold, a little unhappy. She stood in the doorway of the studio, watching her father.

He was at his easel, painting a picture—something for the cover of a book. He was touching up the purple plume on a pirate's hat.

"She comes," he said. "My beautiful

daughter with the dark, bright eyes."

Claudine didn't answer.

"So quiet." He turned to look at her. "So sad?"

"It will go away," she said.

"It will go away sooner if you talk about it." He put down his brush and settled himself on the couch.

She sat beside him. "We're having a play at school."

"And you didn't get a part."

"No, I got one."

"Well, then?"

"There's an angel in the play," Claudine told him. "She comes in at the end and says, 'Glory hallelujah,' or something like that. I wanted to be the angel."

"But somebody else got the part."

"Yes. I could have done it, too. I'd have come in—sort of floaty—with my arms out. I showed Mrs. Adams, but she picked Jennifer Kimball instead."

"Jennifer is the the teacher's pet?"

"No. Actually she likes me better. But Jennifer is blond. Mrs. Adams says she *looks* like an angel."

Father's eyebrows went up. "Where is it written that angels have to be blond?"

Claudine sighed. "I guess it doesn't have to be written. Everybody seems to know it."

"Nonsense." Father went over to his drawing board. He began to draw very fast with crayons.

He held up what he had drawn, a girl with white wings and black hair. She looked like Claudine, and she carried a sign that said: I'M AN ANGEL TOO!

"Show this to Mrs. Adams," he said.

Claudine began to laugh. "No, it's all right. My part is better anyway." She was

looking at the picture. "This is *good*."

"It is rather," he agreed.

And although neither of them knew it, that was the beginning of the angels.

CHAPTER TWO

The Claudine Angel

When Claudine came home from school the next day, the picture was gone from Father's easel.

"Did you finish your pirate?" she asked.

"Not quite," he answered. "I put him away. I'm tired of doing pictures for book covers."

"I thought you liked doing them."

"They pay the bills," he said.

"Is that the only reason you do them?"

"No. I like doing them. But after you've

done a few hundred, you want to do something different." Father was fussing with a wire framework that she had never seen before.

"What is that?" she asked.

"An experiment."

"What will it be?"

"Let's wait and see what happens. When it's ready, I'll surprise you."

He kept the experiment hidden from her.

"Don't look behind the screen," he said.

Within a few days it was finished—a tall, slender angel with widespread wings. She wore a white, flowing robe. Her face was *noble,* and there was a bit of pink in her cheeks. Her hair was black. She was waiting under the skylight when Claudine came home.

Claudine dropped her books and

clasped her hands. "Oh, she's beautiful!"

Father was beaming. "You'd never think she was nearly all wire and cloth and paper, would you? You can lift her with one hand."

"Her hair shines."

"It's an old wig. I dyed it."

"It doesn't look wiggy. She's just perfect."

"A long time ago I wanted to build something on a wire frame, but I couldn't decide what," he said. "You put the angel into my head."

"I'm glad." Claudine was at the telephone, calling the Fieldings.

Don Fielding and his wife, Mary, were their best friends. Claudine and her father had lived with them for a year after Claudine's mother had died. Then Father had said, "We love you, but we're leaving. You've taken care of us long enough."

Mary answered the telephone, and Claudine said, "You've got to come over."

"Dear child, you sound all excited," said Mary. "What *is* it?"

"I can't *tell* you," Claudine said. "You have to *see*."

Don and Mary came over. They stood still when they saw the angel.

"Heavenly, just heavenly!" said Mary.

"Where did you get such an idea?" asked Don.

"From my darling daughter," Father said proudly. "This is my Claudine angel."

Mary was looking into the angel's face. "I do see a little of Claudine. A little of someone else, too."

"Who?" asked Father.

"Laura," said Mary.

Laura was Claudine's mother.

"Yes," said Father. "I never planned it, but somehow it happened."

"It's the best thing you've ever done," said Don. "Let's celebrate."

"Let's have a party for the angel," said Claudine.

It was a joke at first. Then they grew serious.

"We *could* have a party," said Father.

"To introduce the angel to the world," said Don.

"I'll do the invitations," said Claudine. "I'll put 'Come to the Angel Party.' They won't know what it means till they get here."

"Wait, wait." Mary was shaking her head. "This is Friday. Aren't we forgetting something?"

It was Friday, and on Monday she and Don were off to Africa.

"We'll wait till you come back," said Father.

Again Mary shook her head. "It may be months." She was writing a book about Africa, and Don was taking the pictures for it. "If we wait that long, we'll never have the party."

"Have it without us," said Don.

"No," said Claudine.

"No," said Father.

Claudine had been thinking. "Let's have it on Sunday. We'll have all Saturday to get ready. We can do it."

Mary hugged her. "Dear child, I think we can."

CHAPTER THREE

The Party

It was too late to mail the invitations. They invited everyone on the telephone. On Saturday, while Father and Don went to find extra chairs, Claudine and Mary put up decorations. They draped the ceiling with paper streamers. They hung a paper bell just over the angel's head.

Claudine couldn't stop gazing at the angel. "Does she really look like my mother?"

"Not as much as I thought at first," said Mary.

"I try to remember how she looked, but I can't. I was so little when she died. Aunt Lona says she and Mother looked alike. Do you think so?"

"They were both slim and dark. That's about all. Lona used to pretend they were twins, but they never looked alike to me."

"Should we ask her to the party?" Claudine quickly answered her own question. "No, it's a long drive, and—" Suddenly she remembered. Aunt Lona and Mary weren't the best of friends.

"Why doesn't she like you?" asked Claudine.

"I've told you the story," said Mary.

"I know, but I never understood it."

"I was the one who introduced your father to your mother," said Mary. "Lona will never forgive me for that. And she never will forgive him for taking Laura away from her."

"Did she think she could keep her sister with her forever? You can't hold on to a person the way you can hold on to a dish or a table!"

"Some people think you can." Mary was up on a chair. "Hand me a thumbtack, and I'll fix this streamer."

Claudine knew that she was really saying, "Let's talk about something else." Mary didn't much like talking about Aunt Lona.

Claudine handed her a thumbtack and changed the subject. "How long will you be in Africa?"

"We figure on three months, but it could be longer." Mary tacked up the loose streamer and got down off the chair. "I'll tell you something. This is our last trip."

"You always say that."

"This time I mean it. We're getting

tired of running around the world like two old gypsies. We're going to settle down."

"Where?"

"We're thinking about a place in Maine. It's a big old house just outside a town. You can look out and see islands in a bay. And here's the best part. There's room for you and your father."

"Oh, Mary!"

"There'd be a studio for your father and a nice room for you. There! How does that strike you?"

"It sounds like heaven."

"It does, doesn't it?"

They stood there awhile, not saying anything. Claudine began to see it: the big old house on the bay. Father in his new studio. She in her room—a real room and not just a corner with a curtain across it. Mary and Don there all the time and not somewhere halfway around the world.

"Of course, we're not sure we can get the house," said Mary, "so don't mention this to your father. Anyway, he might not like the idea."

"I think he'd love it."

"Don't be too sure. He might think we're trying to do something to help him, and he'd never stand for that. Oh, no. He's a proud one."

"He *is* proud."

"Stubborn," said Mary cheerfully. "Pigheaded."

That was the end of their talk, because the men had come back with the chairs.

🌿 🌿 🌿

The party got off to a fine start. Claudine wore her best dress—red velvet with a white collar—and met people at the door. There were neighbors and artist friends, and there were people she had never seen before, friends of Mary and Don's.

The angel caused a great stir.

"She looks as if she stepped out of a stained-glass window," someone said.

"Do more," said someone else. "They'll make you famous."

There was music. Frankie from the delicatessen down the street had brought his accordion. There was dancing, although there wasn't much room for it. The punch and cold salmon and potato salad were disappearing.

Claudine whispered to Father, "We're running out of food. Can we get more?"

"The delicatessen is closed."

"Maybe if we ask Frankie, he'll open it up for us, and—" She looked at Father then and cried out. His face had gone gray. He was falling.

She pushed a chair toward him. He fell into it.

Mary and Don were there. The room had grown quiet.

Mary said, "I'll call a doctor."

"No!" said Father. "I'll be all right. Give me a minute, and I'll—"

Don told Claudine, "Get some water."

She ran to the kitchen. When she came back, Don and Mary had helped Father into the bedroom. He was on the bed. He seemed to have grown smaller. His eyes were closed tightly as if he were in pain.

"I don't know who his doctor is," said Don.

"I—I don't think he has one," said Claudine.

"Don't call a doctor," said Father.

People were crowding into the bedroom. Don blocked their way. "He needs to rest. I'm sorry, but you'd all better go."

The party broke up quickly. In a little while the studio was empty. Claudine was still holding the glass of water. Her hand was shaking. The water had spilled down the front of her dress.

"We'll stay tonight," said Mary.

"Oh, please do!" Claudine started to say, but Father broke in, "You will not stay. I'm all right."

And it really seemed that he was. His voice was strong again. The awful grayness was gone from his face.

"It was the excitement and not enough air to breathe," he said. "I feel like an idiot. How could I do this to my own party?"

"We'd better stay tonight," said Don.

"Mary can sleep on the couch, and I'll sleep in the big chair."

"If you do, you'll miss your plane in the morning," said Father.

"It doesn't matter," said Don.

"It does to me," said Father. "You're not staying."

So Mary and Don stayed only long enough to clear away the food and straighten up the studio.

By that time, Father was back on his feet. He and Claudine went to the door with Mary and Don.

Mary was crying a little. "I hate leaving you like this."

"It's all right," Father told her. "We have our own guardian angel."

And they all turned to look at the angel standing so calm and lovely in the quiet room.

CHAPTER FOUR

The Four Seasons

Father was not quite as well as he had pretended to be in front of Mary and Don. In the morning he was pale, and he moved so slowly that Claudine was anxious.

"I'm going to stay home from school."

"You are not," he said.

"Yes, I am, and you can't stop me."

He didn't argue. She stayed home from school most of that week. He called her Miss Jennings, his trained nurse. He made a silly cap for her to wear.

"The service here is terrible," he said.

"We do the best we can, sir," she answered.

"I ordered my eggs an hour ago."

"They'll be up in a minute."

He beat on the table with his fist. "I want them *now*."

"If you don't like the way we do things here, you can take your business somewhere else."

"Don't get snippy with me, Miss Jennings. Take that ugly picture off the wall. Bring me my strawberry shortcake. There goes the phone again. Answer it!"

The phone calls were real. One came from Mary and Don just before their plane left. Some were from people asking about the angel.

"They want to know if you're going to do another one," Claudine told him.

"Tell them I'm waiting for my next inspiration," he said.

By the end of the week they were tired of the four walls, tired of the telephone.

"Let's make our escape," he said.

"Are you well enough?"

"Here's a secret. I wasn't sick at all. I just wanted someone to take care of me."

"That's not true. You were sinking fast, and I nursed you back to health."

"Well, now that I've stopped sinking, let's celebrate. How about a picnic?"

A picnic was their favorite way to celebrate. Claudine made cucumber sandwiches, and they took the bus to their favorite park. "It's spring," she said. "It came while we weren't looking."

They had the little green park all to themselves. They walked across it, and there in the middle was the crab-apple tree.

It stood alone, covered with blossoms of the palest pink. The morning light was on it. A few petals were drifting down like snow.

"Here it is, my inspiration," Father said, and Claudine had a sudden picture of what the next angel would be.

❧   ❧   ❧

It was the Angel of Spring.

They went shopping for the white cloth that would be the angel's robe. Father stretched it over a drawing board and began painting on it. She watched as apple blossoms grew under his brush.

"Couldn't I help?" she asked.

"If you want to."

He showed her how to hold the brush. He guided her hand at first. Then he stood back while she painted a blossom by herself.

"Be sure to keep it a *pale* pink."

"But some of the buds were brighter. Every now and then there was a rose color."

"Show me what you mean."

She painted a pale pink bud and tipped it with rose.

He studied it a moment. "I like that. Put in a few more of those touches—not too many—here and here and here."

When the Angel of Spring was finished, there was no waiting for another inspiration. The Angel of Summer came next, in yellows and soft greens.

Then came the Angel of Autumn in fall colors.

"Could she have a leaf in her hand?" asked Claudine, and Father gave the angel a red maple leaf.

Winter was a grave-looking angel with snowflakes around the hem of her robe.

Claudine helped paint them with silver paint.

Now there were five. Five angels in a row along one wall of the studio.

"Which one do you like best?" asked Father.

Claudine couldn't choose. "I really think I like them all the same."

"Don't forget they're partly yours," he said. "You helped with them all."

🌿 🌿 🌿

A man from the museum came by.

"I've been hearing about these," he said, as he walked up and down the row of angels. "I'd like to show them."

"There aren't enough for a show," said Father.

"Yes, there are," said the man.

He took the angels to the museum and

gave them a room to themselves. Each one stood on a separate turntable that turned very slowly. There were moving lights and angel music.

From the first, the show was a success. People flocked to see it. "The show of the year," a newspaper called it.

Claudine heard someone ask Father, "Are the angels for sale?"

"Later I might make some for sale," he said, "but I couldn't sell these."

She squeezed his arm and whispered, "*Thank* you."

The show lasted a month. Then a woman wanted to borrow the angels for her church.

Father looked doubtful. "They're mostly cloth and paper. They're not meant to travel much."

"We'll take good care of them," promised the woman. "Don't you see? A church is where angels belong."

So the angels were moved to the big church downtown. Claudine and her father went to see them. There were two on one side, three on the other.

Claudine said, "Don't you think they're a little too—too—?"

"Spread out? Yes. They get lost in all this space."

"You need to make more."

"I'm thinking about it. Maybe an Angel of the Forest."

"And an Angel of the Sea."

"An Angel of the Storm Clouds, too. Claudine, there's no end to it. We'll have angels everywhere. I'll be the famous Angel Man."

"I'll be his Angel Daughter!"

And they tried to keep from laughing in the quiet church.

CHAPTER FIVE

Aunt Lona

Spring vacation came, time for Claudine to spend a week with Aunt Lona. It was something that had started long ago. Now it had become a family rule, and family rules were hard to break.

Aunt Lona drove in from the country, looking crisp and cool in white linen. She was early. Claudine wasn't quite ready.

"Sit down, Lona," said Father. "Have some coffee."

Aunt Lona refused the coffee, and she

wouldn't sit down. She walked about the studio, her eyes darting.

Claudine went into the corner she called her room. A quarrel was in the air. She could feel it, and she tried to finish packing before it began, but it broke out almost at once.

She heard Aunt Lona say, "How can you live like this?"

"Like what?" asked Father.

"This place is a pigsty."

"It's my studio. I work here."

"It's no place for a child. Claudine doesn't have a proper room. Just a corner with that ratty curtain across it. Her mother must be turning in her grave."

"You'd better stop," said Father.

Aunt Lona kept on. "That child is too thin. She doesn't eat right. I can tell."

"She's *not* too thin. We don't starve here."

"And how on earth can she get her sleep and rest with your friends coming and going day and night?"

"You've always had strange ideas of how we live."

Claudine came out with her suitcase. "I'm ready."

Aunt Lona asked her, on the drive into the country, "Did you hear what your father and I were saying?"

"Some of it," said Claudine.

"Well, you *are* too thin, and there's not much I can do about it in a week. Why can't you stay longer? Next time plan to stay a month."

Claudine didn't answer. How could she tell Aunt Lona that a week was too long and a month would be forever!

🌿   🌿   🌿

She thought a house in the country should be full of light and air. Aunt Lona's was full of gloom. The Chinese rugs were beautiful—and dark. The curtains were heavy and expensive looking—and dark. The rooms were dim and always a little stuffy.

She went outside whenever she could. She walked in the woods at the back of the house. She went to talk with Parsons, the old handyman, who had a room in the stables.

He didn't quite know her at first. He spoke to her in a shy, bumbling sort of way.

"Poor old Parsons," said Aunt Lona. "He was always *slow*."

"He's friendly," said Claudine.

"I'm sure we can find better things for you to do than visiting with Parsons," said Aunt Lona. She talked of having a party for Claudine. "But a week is so short. It's hardly worthwhile making friends."

She took Claudine on long drives. They dined at quaint places. The days were full, but Claudine thought the week would never end. When at last she was back home in the studio, she told her father, "I'll never go away again. Never, never!"

"I tried to call you," he said. "Lona said you were out."

"I was in the woods. She didn't want me to call you back," said Claudine. "She was expecting some important calls, and she didn't want the phone tied up. I started to write you a letter. She said that was ridiculous when I'd be seeing you so soon, so I tore it up."

"What did it say?"

"'Dear Father, I am in the dark dungeon. Please save me.'"

"If I'd gotten that letter, I'd have come to save you. Nothing could have stopped me."

He was putting together another wire framework.

"The Forest Angel?" she asked.

"I think so. But first I have to do something to pay the bills."

Father looked tired. He would paint awhile and rest awhile.

"Sometimes you're a long way off when I talk to you," she said. "Are you all right?"

"Of course I'm all right." He sounded almost cross. "Why shouldn't I be all right?"

He lay on the couch one afternoon. "I have to finish this picture today. If I go to sleep, wake me by three."

She called him at three. He didn't

move, and she gave him a little shake. He lay so still that she was frightened. She ran and got the man downstairs.

He looked at Father and felt his pulse. Then he called the hospital. Two men in white came and took Father away.

CHAPTER SIX

The Brown-Paper Bundles

Aunt Lona came to stay with Claudine. Every day they went to the hospital.

"I'm coming home tomorrow," Father would say. Behind his back, the doctor would shake his head.

One day Father said to Aunt Lona, "You've taken good care of my beautiful daughter. Thank you." He said to Claudine, "The angels are yours."

On the way home she asked Aunt Lona, "What did he mean, the angels are mine?"

Aunt Lona didn't answer.

The next morning they were still in bed when the telephone rang. Aunt Lona went out into the studio to take the call. "Yes," Claudine heard her say. "Yes . . . thank you."

Aunt Lona came back into the bedroom. "That was the hospital. Your father . . ."

"Was he on the phone?" asked Claudine. "Did he want to talk to me?"

"Your father died this morning," said Aunt Lona.

Claudine lay still. The words echoed over and over in her head. For a long time, all she felt was a terrible numbness.

That night, after she had gone to bed, she thought Father was calling her. "What?" she said, before it came to her that she had been dreaming. That was when she began to cry.

Every day more letters and cards came to the studio. Claudine looked at each one. "Nothing from Mary and Don," she said.

"Who?" asked Aunt Lona.

"Mary and Don Fielding. You did let them know, didn't you?"

"Don't forget," said Aunt Lona, "they're in the middle of Africa. It's probably hard for word to get in and out."

"I thought I'd hear by now."

"Don't expect too much of friends. You don't see anyone up here helping us, do you?"

She and Claudine were clearing out the studio. People came for the rugs, the curtains, the furniture. Two girls from an art school carried off Father's painting things. They even took the wire framework that

was the beginning of the last angel. Claudine wondered what it would have been. The Forest Angel? The Angel of the Storm Clouds? No one would ever know.

In the midst of it all, moving men brought in five big brown-paper bundles and leaned them against the wall.

Aunt Lona bit her lip. "I *told* the church to *keep* them."

"No!" cried Claudine. "They're the angels!"

"Listen to me," said Aunt Lona. "They may have been pretty once, but they were flimsy to begin with. They've had their day. The church doesn't want them any longer. The best thing to do is leave them here and—"

"I *won't* leave them!"

They faced each other. Aunt Lona was the first to look away.

When they left for the country, the angels were with them.

CHAPTER SEVEN

The Girls

At Aunt Lona's they went up to Claudine's room together. Aunt Lona threw open the door.

"Surprise!" she said gaily.

Everything had been changed. There was a four-poster bed, a dresser, and a chest of drawers, all new, in dark, gleaming wood. There was new wallpaper with rows of tiny blue flowers and tiny green leaves. There was a green carpet that looked like thick grass.

Claudine was bewildered. "But . . . you haven't been here. How did you do it?"

Now and then Aunt Lona was playful. She was playful now. "Magic," she said.

"How *did* you do it? Really?"

"I made a few phone calls." Aunt Lona looked pleased with herself. "I wanted everything ready when you moved in."

Claudine would never have said so, but the room still looked gloomy. And the bed was too big. It took up half the room.

She said, "I don't know where the angels will go."

"You can see there's no place for them here," said Aunt Lona.

Claudine could see that.

Aunt Lona said briskly, "We'll have Parsons take care of them for now."

Claudine went with the old handyman while he loaded the brown bundles on a wheelbarrow and took them to the stables. She watched him climb the ladder and push them up under the rafters.

"Be careful," she said.

"What are they—mummies?" he asked.

It was a stupid thing to say. For a little while she didn't like him at all. Then she remembered what Aunt Lona had said. Parsons was *slow*.

"I guess you miss your daddy," he said, after he had put away the ladder and wheelbarrow.

"I miss him all the time," she said.

"I must have had a daddy once. A mother, too." He gave a wheezy little laugh. "Now I'm an orphan."

It was odd that she hadn't thought of it before, but she was an orphan, too.

"Well, you've got yourself a good home now," said Parsons. "Stepped right into it, same as I did. I guess we're both lucky. I live right here where my work is."

He showed her his room in the stables. It was a wooden box of a room with nothing in it but a narrow bed and a white plastic chair. The brown-and-yellow cover on the bed looked like a horse blanket.

He pointed to the chair. "She gave me that. I can take it outside of an evening and sit and smoke my pipe."

"That's nice," she said. "I have to go now."

"Stop by again when you've got nothing better to do."

"Thank you, I will."

She did stop a few times because she was sorry for him, because she was lonely. Then she was too busy to think much about him, too busy to be lonely.

Aunt Lona had brought in a tutor to

help Claudine prepare for school. "We'll have to see to it that you hold your own with the other girls," she said.

"Don't worry about it," said Claudine. "I think I can hold my own."

"But you've never been to a school like Mannering. There are certain things you're expected to know. And of course there's more than just your studies. You'll be learning a new way of life. You'll have all those friends, you'll be part of a group, and—"

"I always had friends at school. I had lots of friends," said Claudine. "And I went to a good school. There was nothing wrong with it."

"Now don't ruffle your feathers," Aunt Lona said playfully. "I know I'm not explaining this very well, but your life is different now. When you meet the

Mannering girls, you'll see what I mean."

She gave an afternoon party and invited some of the girls. Courtney and Drew. Stacy and Jessica. Ardith. They were Claudine's age, and they would all be in Mannering School in the fall. They talked alike, Claudine thought. In a way, they looked alike.

Ardith's mother came with Ardith. They were neighbors and lived just on the other side of the woods. They stayed after the others had left.

Aunt Lona asked anxiously, "Do you think it went all right?"

"It went very well," said Ardith's mother.

"They seemed awfully quiet," said Aunt Lona.

"That doesn't mean a thing. They're acquainted now. The ice is broken."

Aunt Lona looked at Claudine. Claudine knew she was expected to say, "I enjoyed the party. Everything was lovely," and she couldn't say it. She was thinking, It was awful, those girls lined up against me, letting me know I'm not one of them and probably won't ever be.

Ardith was watching her. Claudine thought, with a cold feeling down her back, She knows exactly what I'm thinking.

CHAPTER EIGHT

Ardith

Claudine had riding lessons. She rode Aunt Lona's gentle old pony, Candy. She had thought she might enjoy riding. It would give her a chance to be alone, to sort out her feelings about this strange new life. But after the third lesson, Ardith came over to ride with her.

It couldn't have been Ardith's idea. It certainly wasn't Claudine's. Yet here they were, nearly every day, out riding together.

Aunt Lona and Ardith's mother were old friends. It must have been their idea. Claudine and Ardith were supposed to be friends, too.

After one of their rides, Aunt Lona was on the porch when they stopped in front of the house.

"Did you have a good ride?" she asked.

"Yes, thank you," answered Ardith, and she rode away.

"A lovely child," said Aunt Lona. "Not pretty, but terribly bright. I'm glad you're getting on so well."

Claudine turned Candy's head toward the stables.

Aunt Lona asked rather sharply, "You *are* getting on well, aren't you?"

"I don't know," said Claudine. "She seems sort of shut up inside herself. I don't know what to say to her."

"Well, *find* something to say. She may not be like the friends you're used to, but I'm sure you can find something to talk about if you try."

The next time she and Ardith rode together, Claudine told her about Mary and Don. "They were the best friends we had, my father and I. Then they went off to Africa, and I haven't heard from them since."

She told Ardith about her father. "He wasn't a famous artist, but he might have been someday." She even told her about the angels. "They're all wrapped up and hard to get to, but if you'd like to see them—"

"I know about them," said Ardith.

"How do you know?"

"Your aunt told my mother. They're dolls, aren't they?"

"No, they're angels. They're taller than we are, and . . ." Claudine didn't go on. She could see that Ardith wasn't much interested in anything she had said.

A few days later, when they were riding along the edge of the woods, Ardith asked, "Can you come to my house next Friday and spend the night?" She didn't seem much interested in that, either.

"I'll have to ask Aunt Lona."

"She already knows. She and Mother talked about it."

"I'd better ask anyway."

"You don't want to come, do you?"

Claudine hesitated.

"It's too bad when people can't tell each other the truth," said Ardith. "Don't you think so?"

"I suppose it is."

"I'm going to tell you the truth. It

wasn't my idea for you to come over on Friday night. I had to ask because your aunt planned it with my mother. It's so you won't be home on Saturday morning."

"Why—" began Claudine.

"They're playing a trick on you. Your aunt is getting rid of your dolls."

"My dolls? The angels?"

Ardith nodded. "While you're at my house on Saturday morning, a truck is going to come and take them to the dump."

Claudine couldn't remember the ride home, but all at once she was at the stables. She was leaving the pony there. She was running up to the house.

Aunt Lona was in the greenhouse, potting orchids.

"I'll finish this last one, then we'll have

dinner." She smiled. "Did you have a good ride?"

"Are you going to send the angels to the dump?" asked Claudine.

The smile froze on Aunt Lona's face. "Who told you? Was it Parsons? That old fool—"

"Are you?" asked Claudine.

"Yes," said Aunt Lona.

"Without telling me?"

"If I'd told you—if I'd tried to talk to you—you wouldn't have listened. I didn't want to bring those things out in the first place, but you were all upset, and I humored you. It's time I stopped humoring you and helped you grow up. The angels are going. It's dangerous to keep them."

"Dangerous?"

"They could catch fire. And there's just no reason to keep them any longer."

"This is really about my father, isn't it?" said Claudine. "You hated him, didn't you?"

Aunt Lona's face turned a dark, ugly red. "Go to your room!" she said.

CHAPTER NINE

The Night of the Angels

Claudine sat on her bed and watched night come slowly into the room. Through the window she could see the moon shining down on the stables. It was a cold moon.

She went to the head of the stairs and listened. The house was still. She went downstairs and out the back door.

Lights were still on in the stables. Parsons was sitting outside his door, smoking his pipe.

"You can bring down the angels," she told him.

He looked surprised and a little guilty. "I wasn't supposed to get them yet."

"I know, but you can get them now."

He brought the ladder. He climbed up and dragged the bundles out from under the rafters. One by one, he handed them down to her.

"Can we put them on the wheelbarrow?" she asked.

He brought the wheelbarrow. They loaded the bundles across it like logs.

"Where did you want them to go?" he asked.

"I'll show you."

She led the way to the low concrete wall back of the stables. She stood the bundles up on the wall.

"Do you have a knife?" she asked.

He handed her his pocket knife. She cut the wrappings off the bundles until the angels were free.

They had changed. Most of the wings were torn. Some of the robes were wrinkled and stained. But they were beautiful in the moonlight.

She remembered the Claudine Angel on the night of the party, how proud Father had been. She remembered all five—the Claudine Angel and the Four Seasons—in the museum with the music and colored lights. And in the church, where the angels had looked a little lost. She heard herself saying to Father, "You need to make more." She heard him answering, "I'm thinking about it."

She went down the row and touched each angel.

She said to Parsons, "Give me a match."

He took one out of his pocket—a kitchen match. She reached for it. Too late, he tried to draw it back, but she had taken it.

She scratched it on the wall. The flame sprang up. She held it to the nearest angel, then to the others.

They were all on fire. She moved away from the heat.

Parsons was shouting. She hardly heard. As she looked into the brightness, it seemed to her that the air was filled with angels, spreading their wings and rising higher and higher in the sky.

CHAPTER TEN

Letters

It was early morning. Claudine was up and dressed, waiting in her room.

Last night Aunt Lona had said, "We'll talk tomorrow."

Claudine felt tired—she had hardly slept all night—but she was calm.

There was a knock at the door.

"Yes?" she said.

Aunt Lona came in. She looked ill. Her eyes were red, and her mouth twitched a little.

"Breakfast is ready," she said.

"I don't want any," said Claudine.

"Shouldn't you have something?"

"Maybe later. I'm not hungry now."

"Last night . . ." Aunt Lona hesitated. "You said last night you were going away."

"Yes," said Claudine.

"Where will you go?"

"I don't know."

"What will you do?"

"I don't know," Claudine said again. "If I could, I'd go to Mary and Don."

"I rather thought you'd say that." Aunt Lona went out. In a little while she was back with three letters in her hand. She held them out.

Claudine took them. They were addressed to her. Two had foreign stamps. One had a Maine postmark. In the upper left-hand corner of each envelope were the names, *Mary and Don Fielding*.

"You can see they went to your old address," said Aunt Lona. "They were sent on to you here."

Claudine turned the letters over in her hands. They had been opened.

She looked into Aunt Lona's face. "Why did you do this? Why didn't you give them to me?"

"Because . . ." Aunt Lona looked away.

"They were mine, and you opened them and kept them," said Claudine. "Why did you do it?"

"Because Mary and Don Fielding wanted to take you away. They were always there, waiting to take you away."

"Why didn't you let them?" Claudine was holding the letters close to her. "Why didn't you, Aunt Lona?"

"I wanted to keep you. I *thought* I

wanted to keep you. Now I can see we never had much of a future together." Aunt Lona sounded weary and cold. "You saw it before I did, didn't you?"

She was gone.

Claudine sat on the bed and looked at her letters. Two were from Africa. They were old. The third—the one from Maine—was new, in Mary's small, round handwriting. She glanced through it quickly. "Finished in Africa . . . getting settled here . . . your father. It will never be the same without him. I think he would have loved it here. I think *you* will love it . . . pine trees . . . such blue skies and blue water . . . Where are you? Let us know, and we . . ."

On the last page she found it—the telephone number.

She went downstairs. She was running.

She was on the telephone. A singing came over the wires, then a sound like the ocean, then a voice, faint and far away.

"Mary!" she cried.

And the voice was saying, "Child! Dear child!"

About the Author

Clyde Robert Bulla was born on a farm near King City, Missouri. He attended a one-room school where he wrote his first stories. He continued to write during the years when he worked on his hometown newspaper. Now he lives in Los Angeles, devoting most of his time to writing. He has written more than seventy books for young readers. He travels when he gets a chance.

About the Illustrator

Julia Noonan's art has graced everything from fruit juice labels to magnificently glowing picture books. Two years in a row, with 1991's *The Shut-Eye Train* and 1992's *Twinkle, Twinkle, Little Star,* her work was selected as an offering of the Literary Guild. She lives in Brooklyn, New York.